THE SAME BUT DIFFERENT TOO

Karl Newson & Kate Hindley

nosy crow

I am me,
and you are you.

We're the same,
but different too.

I like breakfast.

So do you.

But I can't drink
the way you do!

I am big.

You are
small.

I am short.

You are tall.

I am happy.

You are too!

I can't climb as
high as you.

I am
friendly.

You are
gruff.

I am
gentle.

You are
rough.

I am playful.　　　　You are too.

I can't hide as well as you.

I am
hot.

You are cold.

I am
young.

You are
old.

I am
hungry.

You are too.

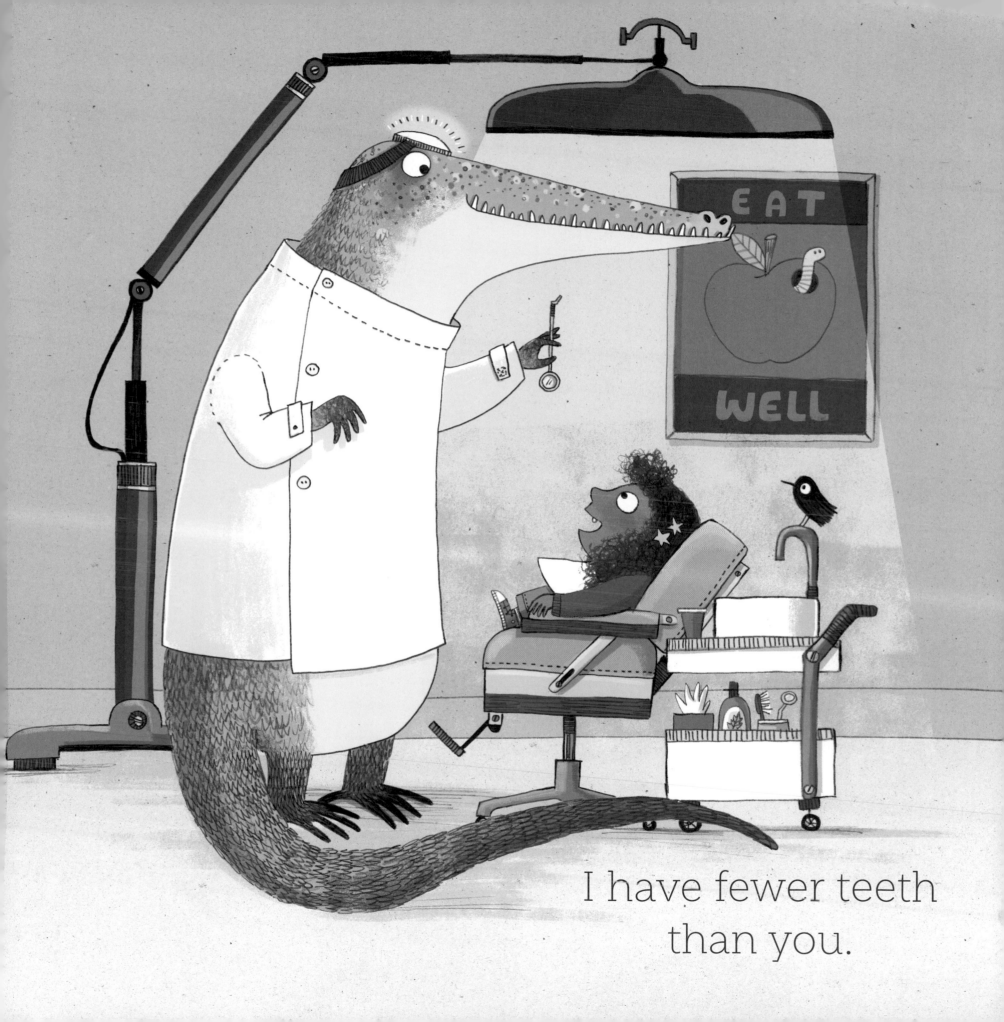

I have fewer teeth
than you.

I am
fast.

You are
slow.

I am wet.   You are too.

I can splash
and swim
like you.

I am
quiet.

You are
loud.

I'm alone.

You're in
a crowd.

I am
listening.   You are too.

I love stories.
So do you.

Now I'm
sleepy.

You are too.

Goodnight me and . . .

...goodnight you.